Rain or Shine

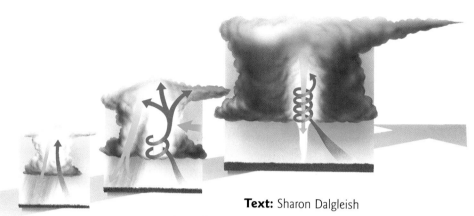

Text: Sharon Dalgleish
Consultant: Richard Whitaker, Senior Meteorologist,
Bureau of Meteorology, Sydney, Australia

This edition first published 2003 by
MASON CREST PUBLISHERS INC.
370 Reed Road
Broomall, PA 19008

© Weldon Owen Inc.
Conceived and produced by
Weldon Owen Pty Limited

Library of Congress Cataloging-in-Publication Data
on file at the Library of Congress
ISBN: 1-59084-168-9

Printed in Singapore.
1 2 3 4 5 6 7 8 9 06 05 04 03

CONTENTS

IT'S COLD OUTSIDE

If you walk through fog, you are really walking through a cloud. During the day, heat from the Sun sinks into the ground. If it is a clear night, with little or no wind, the heat escapes back into space. As the ground gets colder, moisture in the air condenses to form fog. If it is very cold, the moisture freezes to make tiny ice crystals called frost. If it gets colder still, everything will be covered in thick ice.

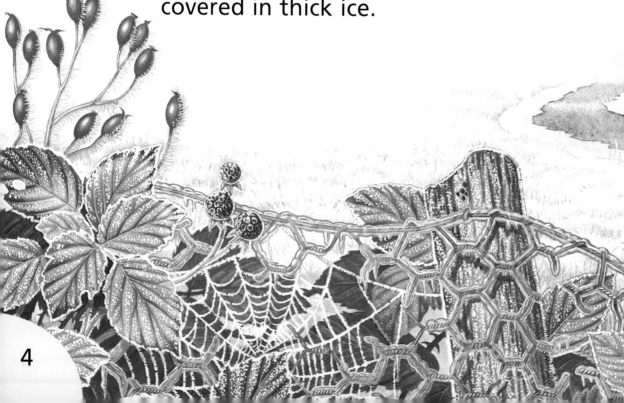

DID YOU KNOW?

If the temperature stays very cold for a long time, even water that is dripping can freeze into icicles.

Clouds are masses of water droplets and ice crystals floating in the sky. If the conditions are right, it will rain, hail, or even snow.

Rain
Tiny water droplets collect around small ice crystals until they get heavy and fall.

MAKING RAIN

1 Find a long metal spoon with a wooden handle. Place it in the freezer for a few minutes. Ask an adult to boil some water.

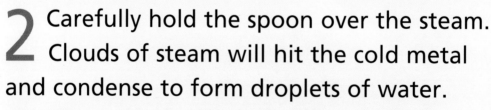

2 Carefully hold the spoon over the steam. Clouds of steam will hit the cold metal and condense to form droplets of water.

3 When the droplets get big and heavy, they will fall. It's raining on your kettle!

Snow

When the air temperature is very cold, the ice crystals don't have time to melt before they reach the ground.

Hail

Strong upward air currents cause extra layers of ice to build up around small ice crystals, which then drop from the sky.

7

The Arctic and Antarctic regions are so cold that they are always covered in snow and ice. Even places close to the equator can be covered in snow. Mount Kilimanjaro is Africa's highest mountain. It wears a cap of snow all year round.

Iceberg
These floating castles of ice are even bigger than they look. Only about one-ninth can be seen above the water. That's just the tip of the iceberg!

Igloo
The Inuit people live in the Arctic region. Some still build igloos from slabs of ice. Inside it's warm and sheltered.

Mountain Snow

High mountains, such as these, are covered in snow throughout the year.

AMAZING!

Snowflakes are clusters of ice crystals. No two snowflakes are exactly the same. When it is warmer, the crystals are smaller and more needlelike.

9

WIND

You may not notice it, but the air around us is always on the move. The turning of the Earth and the heat from the Sun cause areas of high and low air pressure to form. Wind flows from high-pressure areas to low-pressure areas. The picture below shows how a sea breeze forms in this way.

Moving Up
Air warms during the day and rises.

Moving Across
The warm air spreads out.

Going Down
Air drops over cooler areas, such as the sea.

Wind Blows
Cool air from the sea fills the gap left by the rising warm air.

MEASURING WIND

What you need
- 2 drinking straws
- pen
- 4 disposable cups
- tape
- pencil with an eraser on the end
- 1 pin

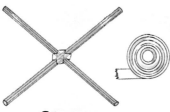

Step one

Step two

1 Make an X shape with the straws. Tape them together.

2 Draw a stripe around one of the cups. Tape a cup onto each end of the straws. All the cups should face the same way.

3 Put a pin through the straws and then into the eraser on the end of the pencil. Take your wind measurer out into the wind. Count how often the striped cup turns around in one minute.

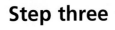

Step three

11

LIGHTNING BOLTS

On hot, humid days, opposite electrical charges can build up in clouds. When the difference between these charges becomes very large, a huge electrical spark—the lightning bolt—is created. At the same time, the heat from the lightning causes the air to expand suddenly. This makes a clap of thunder.

Types of Lightning
1. cloud-to-air lightning
2. lightning within the cloud
3. cloud-to-cloud lightning
4. cloud-to-ground lightning

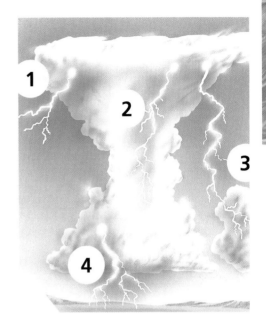

AMAZING!

At this very moment
2,000 thunderstorms are
taking place around the
Earth. There are about
20,000 each day!

WILD WEATHER

The strongest winds on Earth are tornadoes. A tornado is a twisting whirlwind that speeds across the ground. A cyclone is a giant, spinning wind and rainstorm that begins over tropical oceans. It can even be more than one storm joined together. Severe cyclones are called hurricanes in the United States of America and typhoons in parts of Asia.

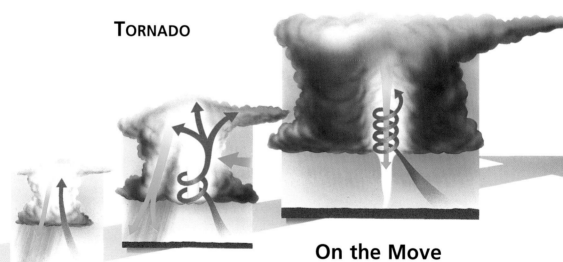

TORNADO

Beginning
Wild winds develop in thunderstorm clouds.

Spinning Out
The winds cause the warm air to twist faster and faster.

On the Move
The funnel of twisting air can produce winds of 200 miles (320 km) per hour.

CYCLONE

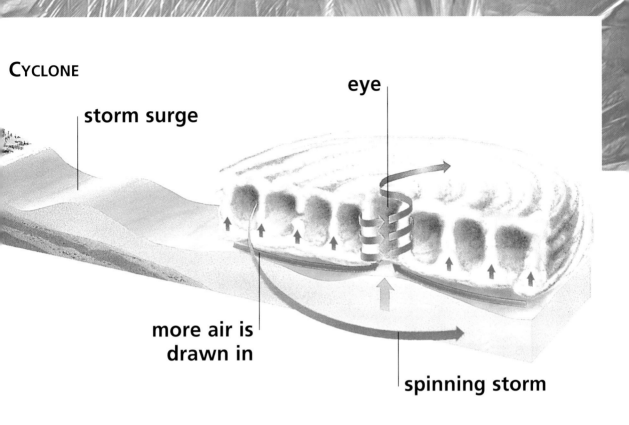

storm surge

eye

more air is drawn in

spinning storm

Storm Damage

A cyclone (left) is very destructive, and a tornado can flatten buildings (above).

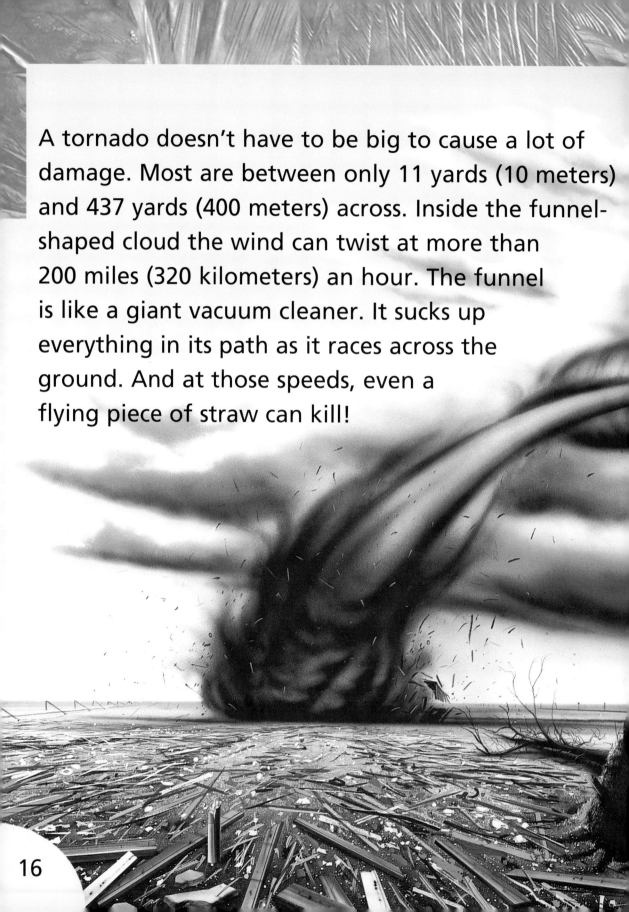

A tornado doesn't have to be big to cause a lot of damage. Most are between only 11 yards (10 meters) and 437 yards (400 meters) across. Inside the funnel-shaped cloud the wind can twist at more than 200 miles (320 kilometers) an hour. The funnel is like a giant vacuum cleaner. It sucks up everything in its path as it races across the ground. And at those speeds, even a flying piece of straw can kill!

DID YOU KNOW?

Kansas, Oklahoma, and Missouri are known as "Tornado Alley." There are more tornadoes here each year than anywhere else on Earth.

July/August/September

April/May/June

January/February/March

Colored Light

Sunlight is a mixture of different colors. We can see these colors when we see a rainbow. Rays of sunlight pass through raindrops and are reflected and bent from inside the drops. We see the reflection as a band of colors.

RAINBOWS

The sky can put on a great special effects show. One of its most colorful displays is a rainbow. Rainbows occur during showers or thunderstorms. To see a rainbow, the Sun must be low in the sky and you must be between it and the rain.

Weather Wonder

For a rainbow to occur, there has to be sunlight and rain at the same time. Then the sunlight is reflected in millions of falling raindrops.

Seeing Double

Sometimes, the light is bent twice inside each raindrop. Then you see two rainbows—but the colors are reversed.

CLOUDS

Clouds form when moist air rises. As the air cools, tiny droplets of water form. This is called condensation. It takes hundreds of millions of water droplets and ice crystals to make one cloud. Clouds look white because the water droplets reflect light. When a cloud gets heavy with droplets, not as much light can pass through it. This makes the cloud look dark.

The Water Cycle
Water moves between the oceans, the atmosphere, and the land in a never-ending cycle.

From Above

We give clouds their names depending on how high they are above the ground. These clouds are called stratocumulus. They are among the lowest clouds.

Cirrostratus
High-level, layered clouds. Cold weather might be on the way.

Watching the clouds can tell you important information about the weather. First, try to identify the shape: fluffy or layered. Then try to figure out the height from the ground.

Cumulonimbus
These are the clouds that make thunderstorms. They can tower 11 miles (18 kilometers) into the sky and hold 100,000 tons of water.

Cumulus
Low-level, fluffy clouds. Enjoy a warm sunny day.

Cirrocumulus
High-level, fluffy clouds.
The weather might change.

Cirrus
High-level, wispy clouds
made of ice crystals. It might
become windy or there
could be a thunderstorm.

Altostratus
Mid-level, layered
clouds. Look out for
heavy rain or snow.

Altocumulus
Mid-level, fluffy clouds.
There might be light rain.

Stratus
Low-level, layered clouds.
Drizzle could be on the way.

Stratocumulus
Low-level, lumpy clouds.
It could be a clear night.

23

Weather Balloon
This travels high into the atmosphere to record the weather.

Instrument Box
Instruments that measure temperature and humidity are kept in here.

Sunshine Recorder
This keeps track of the hours of sunlight in one day.

Wind Measurer
This measures wind speed near the evaporation pan.

Recording Rain Gauge
This records the total amount of rainfall.

Evaporation Pan
This records how fast water evaporates.

Rain Gauge
This measures rainfall over 24 hours.

WEATHER WATCHING

Do you listen to the weather forecast on the radio or TV? The weather is always changing. Weather stations around the world gather information about these changes. All these reports are then put together to make the weather forecasts you hear.

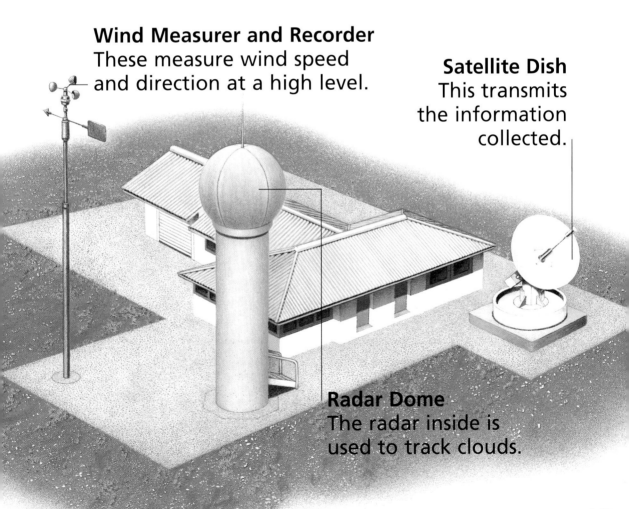

Wind Measurer and Recorder
These measure wind speed and direction at a high level.

Satellite Dish
This transmits the information collected.

Radar Dome
The radar inside is used to track clouds.

HUMIDITY

Humidity is the amount of water vapor or moisture in the air. If the humidity is high, you feel hotter. This is because water doesn't evaporate easily when it is humid. This means sweat, which normally helps cool the body, doesn't evaporate quickly. It stays on the skin longer and makes you feel hotter. Humidity is measured with either a hygrometer or a wet and dry bulb thermometer.

Rain Forest
Plants grow well in a rain forest because the air is very moist, or humid.

MEASURING HUMIDITY

This is a wet and dry bulb thermometer. One bulb is wrapped in a wet cloth. If the air is dry, evaporation cools the wet bulb. If the air is humid, the two readings are almost the same.

hot and sticky

Desert

A desert can be the same temperature as a rain forest, but it is hard for plants to survive there. The heat is very dry.

WORLD CLIMATES

Even though the weather changes from day to day, the pattern of weather in a region is usually similar. This pattern of weather is called the climate. Different parts of the world can be divided into broad climatic zones.

Tropical
These regions are hot and wet.

Mountain
These regions are cold, wet, and windy.

Polar
These regions are extremely cold all year.

Temperate
These regions have four distinct seasons.

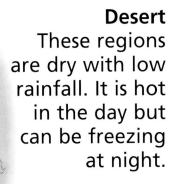

Desert
These regions are dry with low rainfall. It is hot in the day but can be freezing at night.

GLOSSARY

atmosphere The thin layer of gases that surrounds planets such as the Earth.

condensation The changing of water from a vapor to a liquid.

equator An imaginary line around the world that lies halfway between the North and South Poles.

evaporation The changing of water from a liquid to vapor.

eye The small calm area at the center of a cyclone.

vapor A gaslike substance. It can be changed into liquid or solid forms.

INDEX

PICTURE AND ILLUSTRATION CREDITS

BOOKS IN THIS SERIES